MCR

MCR

FEB 1 2 2007

EVANSTON PUBLIC LIBRARY

P9-CSB-010

JPicture Tafur.N
Tafuri, Nancy.
Blue Goose /

BLUE

SIMON & SCHUSTER BOOKS FOR YOUNG READERS
An imprint of Simon & Schuster Children's Publishing Division
1230 Avenue of the Americas, New York, New York 10020
Copyright © 2008 by Nancy Tafuri
All rights reserved, including the right of
reproduction in whole or in part in any form.
SIMON & SCHUSTER BOOKS FOR YOUNG READERS is a
trademark of Simon & Schuster, Inc.
Book design by Tom Daly
The text for this book is set in Journal Bold.
The illustrations for this book are rendered in
brush pen, watercolor pencils, gouache, and ink.
Manufactured in China
10 9 8 7 6 5 4 3 2 1
Library of Congress Cataloging-in-Publication Data
Tafuri, Nancy.
Blue Goose / Nancy Tafuri. — 1st ed.
p. cm.
Summary: When Farmer Gray goes away for the day, Blue Goose,
Red Hen, Yellow Chick, and White Duck get together and paint
their black-and-white farm.
ISBN-13: 978-1-4169-2834-8 (hardcover)
ISBN-10: 1-4169-2834-0 (hardcover)
[1. Domestic animals—Fiction. 2. Farm life—Fiction. 3. Color—Fiction.] I. Title.
PZ7.T117Bl 2008
[E]—dc22   2006038368

first
edition

For Rallou,
my friend who loves color

GOOSE

Nancy Tafuri

Simon & Schuster Books for Young Readers

New York   London   Toronto   Sydney

EVANSTON PUBLIC LIBRARY
CHILDREN'S DEPARTMENT
1703 ORRINGTON AVENUE
EVANSTON, ILLINOIS 60201

While Farmer Gray was away, Blue Goose, Red Hen, Yellow Chick, and White Duck decided to paint their barnyard.

White Duck painted the fence white.

And Yellow Chick painted all the flowers yellow.

Red Hen painted
the barn red.

Blue Goose painted the roof blue.

Blue Goose and Red Hen poured blue and red together to paint the doors purple.

Red Hen helped Yellow Chick mix red
and yellow to paint the shutters orange.

Blue Goose and

White Duck painted
the sky light blue.

Then Yellow Chick and Blue Goose
made green to paint the grass and trees.

They thought,
and thought,
and thought,
until—

Duck climbed on Goose.
Hen climbed on Duck.
Chick climbed on Hen,
and Chick painted
the sun yellow!

"What about the tractor?" cried Chick.

Red Hen painted it
just in the nick of time.

"It's finished," shouted Blue Goose, Red Hen,

The barnyard was filled with color.

"SURPRISE!"
to their Farmer Gray.

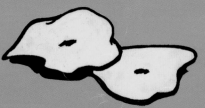

And when it was time for bed, what did Goose do?

She painted everything blue—

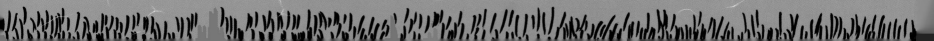

except for the moon.